The Stable Where Jesus Was Born

by RHONDA GOWLER GREENE

illustrated by SUSAN GABER

✳

ALADDIN PAPERBACKS
New York London Toronto Sydney Singapore

First Aladdin Paperbacks edition October 2002
Text copyright © 1999 by Rhonda Gowler Greene
Illustrations copyright © 1999 by Susan Gaber

ALADDIN PAPERBACKS
An imprint of Simon & Schuster
Children's Publishing Division
1230 Avenue of the Americas
New York, NY 10020

Also available in an Atheneum Books for Young Readers hardcover edition.
Designed by Michael Nelson
The text of this book was set in Guardi Roman.
Printed in Hong Kong
2 4 6 8 10 9 7 5 3 1

The Library of Congress has cataloged the hardcover edition as follows:
Greene, Rhonda Gowler.
The stable where Jesus was born / by Rhonda Gowler Greene;
Illustrated by Susan Gaber.—1st ed
p. cm
Summary: Rhyming verse introduces the people who appear in the story of
the birth of Christ and describes the setting of this event.
ISBN 0-689-81258-2 (hc)
1. Jesus ChristóNativity—Juvenile literature. [1. Jesus Christ—Nativity. 2.
Bible stories—N.T.] I. Gaber, Susan, ill. II. Title.
BT315.2.G7347   1999
232.92—dc21   97-39129   CIP   AC

ISBN 0-689-85350-5 (Aladdin pbk.)

For Matt
⁓ R. G. G.

To Joanne
⁓ S. G.

This is the stable where Jesus was born.

⚹

This is the cow in the sweet-smelling hay,
the cat and her kittens and three mice at play,
that lived in the stable where Jesus was born.

⚹

This is the mother, Mary by name,
the mother of Jesus she became,
who sat near the cow in the sweet-smelling hay.

This is the father, Joseph, so tall,
who cared for the baby and animals all,
but mostly the mother, Mary by name.

These are the shepherds who came in the night,
who left flocks of sheep in their hurry and flight
and wished well the father, Joseph, so tall.

This is the angel who said, "Fear not!"
who spoke of a birth in a glorious spot
and sent fast the shepherds who came in the night.

This is the town called Bethlehem
where families gathered and filled every inn,
beheld by the angel who said, "Fear not!"

This is the earth all round and bright
that glimmered with hope that first Christmas night
at news from a town called Bethlehem.

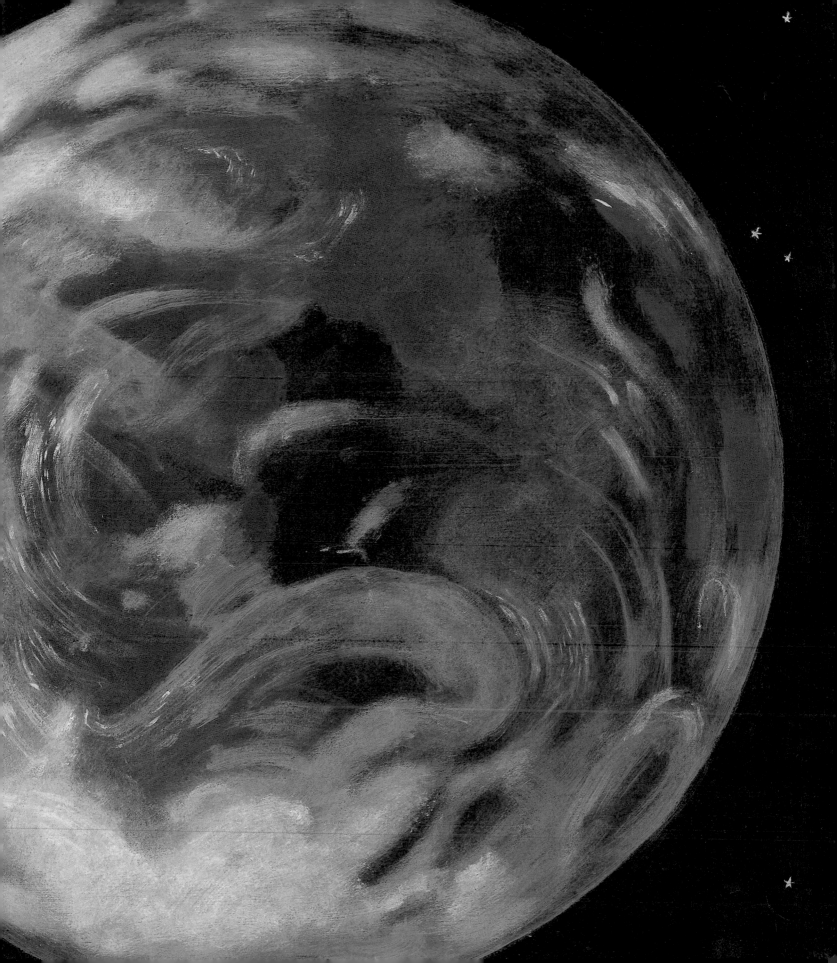

This is the baby in swaddling clothes,
the small precious baby, the one whom God chose
to come to the earth all round and bright
that glimmered with hope that first Christmas night

at news from a town called Bethlehem
where families gathered and filled every inn,

beheld by the angel who said, "Fear not!"
who spoke of a birth in a glorious spot

and sent fast the shepherds who came in the night,
who left flocks of sheep in their hurry and flight

✄

and wished well the father, Joseph, so tall,
who cared for the baby and animals all,

✄

⚭

but mostly the mother, Mary by name,
the mother of Jesus she became,

⚭

᪲

who sat near the cow in the sweet-smelling hay,
the cat and her kittens and three mice at play,

᪲

ॐ

that lived in the stable where Jesus was born.

ॐ